Gift Ded

D1026621

They say laughter is the best medicine.

Yo mama needs no reminders to take that medicine every single day.

Given to: _____

(Name of yo mama or the other lucky person you're giving this to.)

Date: _____

(If it's Mother's Day today, please don't procrastinate so much next time.)

From: _____

(Your name goes here.)

To the giver: please use the check boxes ☐ to mark the jokes you think will resonate most for the fortunate recipient.

To the mama/recipient: if they didn't follow instructions, please remind them when they visit (Which better be soon).

Feel free to write a heart-warming note below.

Here are some helpful words you could use:
thanks, love, remember, taught, appreciate, memories, wise...

Yo Mama's So...

Amazing!

Yo Mama's So…

Amazing!

101 Yo Mama Jokes
You'll Want to Tell Your Mother

by
Joshua Swenson and Gibson Grey

illustrations by
Megan Speirs Mack

Disclaimers

* All mothers appearing in this work are fictitious, but based on an amalgamation of all mothers in general in all of their awesomeness. Any resemblance to your own mother or any specific mother is purely coincidental, though—when positive—also likely accurate. Please accept these coincidental similarities with our best compliments. We believe the best of all mothers.

** Mothers (hereafter known as "mamas") are not assumed nor required to be perfect, though they are assumed to be plenty close enough, especially yo mama.

*** If you manage to read through this book without laughing much, please discuss with yo mama why you didn't inherit more of her excellent sense of humor.

Yo Mama's So… *Amazing!*

Published by Book Tree Publishing, LLC
www.booktree.org

Published 2021

ISBN: 9798732749182

DEDICATION

To Meagan, the *amazing* mama of our children
  my wonderful mama, Valerie,
    Lana, my fabulous mama-in-law,
      and all the awesome grandmamas in our family tree.

-Joshua Swenson

To my wife, my mother, her mother, and my grandmother
who adopted my dad.

-Gibson Grey

To my mama, Heidi, a bold, fiercely loyal woman who I'm
forever grateful to have on my team. To my mama-in-law,
Becky, who raised my best friend. And to my
GRANDmamas, Laurette and Jeana, who make me belly
laugh, be it intentionally or otherwise. They are reliable
sources of happiness!

-Megan Speirs Mack

CONTENTS

INTRODUCTION

Who needs an introduction less than yo mama?

Mothers—who as a group have done more for humanity than any other—are somehow at the receiving end of so much unworthy humor. What did yo mama do to be so deserving?

According to reliable Internet scholars with plenty of free time on their hands, the sordid history of the rude yo mama joke may stretch back as far as 3,500 years to ancient Babylon. William Shakespeare himself was known to have indulged in (i.e., stooped to) such humor, and millions of otherwise good kids have followed in those ignoble Babylonian and Shakespearean footsteps ever since.

The idea for this book was sparked in 2015 at one of the most notorious hotspots for this crass class of humor: scout camp. I was up at Camp Baldwin near Mt. Hood in Oregon, working hard as an assistant scoutmaster with our scouts to learn key life skills such as how to have fun with fire without burning down a forest, how to not fall off a horse, and how to shoot arrows at a target instead of your assistant scoutmaster. (You can imagine why these life skills need to be learned at a distance from most mothers.)

To my disappointment, I found that the time between all of these character-building experiences was too often filled with yo mama jokes, and not the kind you'll find in the pages that follow. No, these normally upstanding boys on their way to manhood were trading the most dreadful insults against their respective mothers.

I'm not saying I didn't laugh. Truthfully, it's hard not to sometimes, but amidst those guilty laughs the idea was born. What if there were yo mama jokes that were both funny *and* nice to mothers? And what if they were funny enough that my scouts might actually tell them to each other on their way to their next class on "playing safely with sharp objects"? That *would* be something.

After all, there's plenty of comedic material in motherhood; anyone who has embarked on the journey of raising a human from a single cell to adulthood knows there's *a lot* to laugh about. On top of that, there's plenty of humor to be had in playing up the many strengths of mothers and maybe poking a little fun at their offspring while we're at it.

Our hope for this book is that it will make you laugh and that your laughter will be magnified by shared memories. For those that bought the print version, please use these check boxes ☐ and write in the margins to mark and personalize your copy for the jokes that will resonate most for you and yo mama.

So, here's to mothers who literally, figuratively, and resiliently shape the world one human at a time. And here's to yo mama, who is responsible for so much of the best in you.

-Joshua Swenson

☐ Yo mama's a superhero. She even still wears a cape sometimes. To keep her identity a secret, she wears the cape backwards and calls it an apron.

☐ Yo mama loves you so much she prepared 22,000 meals for you by the time you went off to college. Think about that the next time you're deciding on a $5 Mother's Day gift.

☐ Yo mama's so fearless she taught you how to drive.

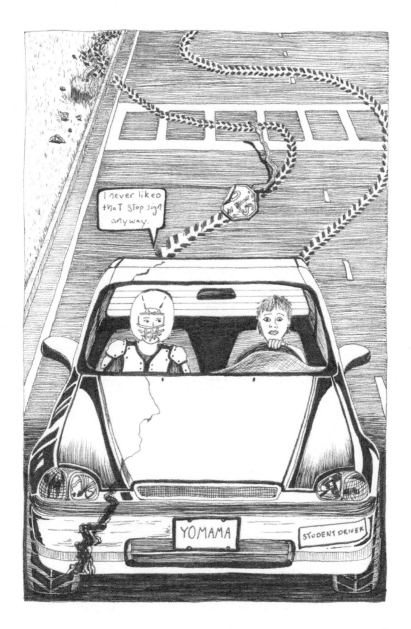

☐ Yo mama's so tough she was recruited by Nick Fury.

☐ Yo mama's so smart she could always learn anything she wants and then learn it all over again when it's time to help you with it for homework.

☐ Yo mama's so thoughtful that she was always been able to send the perfect gift on time even before Amazon existed.

(but now that she's gone Prime, she's never going back!)

☐ Yo mama's so smart that Harvard sent her diploma with her acceptance letter to save on postage.

☐ Yo mama's so energetic that Tesla tried to patent her to use for their batteries.

☐ Yo mama's into extreme sports. How else would you describe wrestling a five-year-old out of her favorite PJs and into clothes that match for picture day?

☐ When yo mama visited Mt. Rushmore, the maintenance workers asked her to hold still so they could add her face to the monument.

She declined saying that she had come on vacation to "rush less".

☐ If yo mama were a professional chef, her food would stay exactly the same. She'd just get paid and thanked more.

☐ Yo mama was so patient with you at the movie theater that she should have been listed in the movie credits.

☐ Yo mama's right that it's not OK for you to have cookies for breakfast before school.

She's also right that it *is* OK for her to have cookies for breakfast after the bus picks you up.

☐ They say that we'll never have peace in the Middle East, but that's only because nobody has taken one of yo mama's pies to the negotiations.

☐ Yo mama's so determined that she never gives up on lost causes... even when they're not very self-aware.

(Hint, hint.)

☐ Yo mama's so optimistic that her glass is always half full. And, because she likes to share that optimism with you, your voicemail is always half full too.

☐ Yo mama is your best therapist for two big reasons:

1. She's the most affordable.

2. She can skip all that "tell me about your mother" nonsense and get straight to the point.

☐ Even though your baby teeth would eventually fall out, yo mama still helped you brush them daily. Kind of like how she washed her hair daily even knowing you'd eventually make it fall out too.

☐ Yo mama's so musical they sometimes call her "Yo-Yo Mama". Rumor has it she taught Yo-Yo Ma everything he know-know ma's about cello.

☐ Yo mama's so beautiful that when she went to Disneyland, all the princesses lined up to take pictures with her.

☐ Yo mama's so right that she doesn't have any opinions of her own.

   She only has facts of her own.

☐ Yo mama is a brilliant general; she may not have chosen to win every battle with you, but she definitely won the war.

☐   There's a simple solution to the political mess we're in: we need to put yo mama on the ballot. Then we'd finally have a candidate we could all agree on.

☐ Yo mama's so positive that when she talks on the phone it recharges the battery.

☐ Yo mama's so loving that she's worked tirelessly for years with only one vacation day per year: Mother's Day.

You only found out later in life that she was also moonlighting as the Tooth Fairy, the Easter Bunny, and Santa Claus.

☐ Before she had you, yo mama had one great career going. Now she's got at least 14: teacher, chef, nurse, housekeeper, journalist, referee, chauffeur, life coach, interior designer, human resources specialist, judge, psychologist, personal shopper, stylist, etc.

☐ When yo mama went back to work, she was able to add a whole page to her résumé about working under pressure and dealing with demanding customers.

☐   Yo mama's so good at saving money her bank calls her a hoarder.

☐ Yo mama's so wise that her two cents are worth twenty bucks any day.

☐ Yo mama's such a patient investor that even her investments in you have started paying dividends.

☐   Yo mama's garden is so nice that weeds pull themselves and run to the neighbors.

☐   Yo mama's house is so clean that you had a 5-hour rule.

☐ Yo mama's house is so clean you could perform minor surgery on her countertop… and she has.

☐ Yo mama's so organized that when she threw away things that didn't "spark joy", the next morning she found Marie Kondo going through her trash trying to figure out her secrets.

☐ Yo mama's cookies are so good that when she gives some to the neighbors they ask her for her recipe… and her autograph.

☐ Yo mama's advice is so good they use tiny pieces of her journal to make fortune cookies.

☐ A picture is worth a thousand words. A picture of yo mama is worth a thousand libraries.

☐ Yo mama's so well-read she takes a truck to the library and says "fill 'er up".

☐ Yo mama's so smart she can watch 60 minutes in half an hour.

☐ Yo mama's so strategic that when you play board games she can find a way to lose fast enough to still get you to bed on time.

☐ Yo mama's so proud of you she brags about you to the cashier at Target... before shopping.

☐ Yo mama's the most generous landlord you've ever had, it even started with nine months of free womb and board.

☐ Yo mama's so wise that when Supreme Court judges argue with each other, they appeal to her.

☐   Yo mama met Chuck Norris once. After an epic staredown, Chuck Norris promised to stop exaggerating so much on the Internet.

☐   Yo mama also met Chuck Norris' mama. They have a lot in common and keep in touch… at their weekly kickboxing class.

☐ Yo mama's so passive aggressive that she "thinks this book was cute and hopes you kept the receipt".

☐ Yo mama's so patient that even a kid like you turned out decent.

☐ Yo mama's so frugal... except with your kids for some reason.

39

☐ Yo mama has such a good memory she can still recall that thank-you note you didn't send her in 2011.

☐ Yo mama's personality is so magnetic that she attracts all of the following: other people's children, new friends, compliments, strangers looking for advice, small collectible figurines, birds to her yard, etc.

☐ Yo mama was in a parade once. And as far as you can tell, she's never been out of it. She's always smiling and waving at everyone.

☐ Yo mama's so nurturing that her hugs contain 10 essential vitamins and minerals.

☐ Yo mama's so flexible she can still do the splits after all these years. She just needs bananas and ice cream to do them now.

43

☐ Yo mama can time travel. No, seriously. How else could she remember where she was for the moon landing and still be 35?

☐ Yo mama's so original that she taught Colonel Sanders how to make chicken. And no, she's not that old. I already told you she can time travel.

☐ In a recent survey of the best places to live for young adults, the top three included Austin, Texas; Portland Oregon; and yo mama's basement. Yo mama's basement edged out the competition with its fine cuisine and its clear victory in the "most affordable" category.

☐ As she has aged gracefully, yo mama has become better at finding the silver lining. She often finds it while doing her hair.

☐ Yo mama's so environmentally conscious that when she hugs a tree, the tree hugs her back.

☐ Yo mama's so creative that if she hadn't created you, you wouldn't exist.

☐ Yo mama just wants to take 34 more pictures of you before you go.

☐ Yo mama's so dedicated she stayed right by your side until you finished potty training. And you were so sweet to try to return the favor and never let her go to the bathroom alone again.

☐ Yo mama's so giving she gave up over a thousand hours of sleep just during the first year of your life. Good thing she's also so forgiving that she wasn't jealous when you slept six thousand hours that same year.

☐ Yo mama knows that actions speak louder than words. That's why when she told you to go to bed, she fell asleep before you did.

☐   You locked yo mama in her room once. Somehow she couldn't get the door unlocked for two hours.

And you heard snoring.

☐   Like Anna Lee Fisher who became the first mother in space in 1984, yo mama is willing to go to similar lengths to get an uninterrupted nap.

☐ Yo mama's so smart she taught you how to speak a language when you were only a baby.

☐ Yo mama's so talented she could put on a whole talent show all by herself, but she'd rather sit in the crowd and clap for you.

☐   Yo mama gets up so early her rooster

wears earplugs.

☐ Yo mama's so talented she could have been on Broadway. But then she picked a job that's even more full of drama... and became yo mama.

☐ Yo mama's so fashionable that when she went to the carpet store, they would only sell her red carpet.

☐ In your house, I think you should rename Alexa to "yo mama" because she's really the one who's got all the answers.

☐ Helen of Troy's face may have launched a thousand ships but yo mama has shipped a thousand lunches with you to school. And she's prettier than Helen too.

☐ Yo mama's such a catch that yo daddy gave up his fishing license for good.

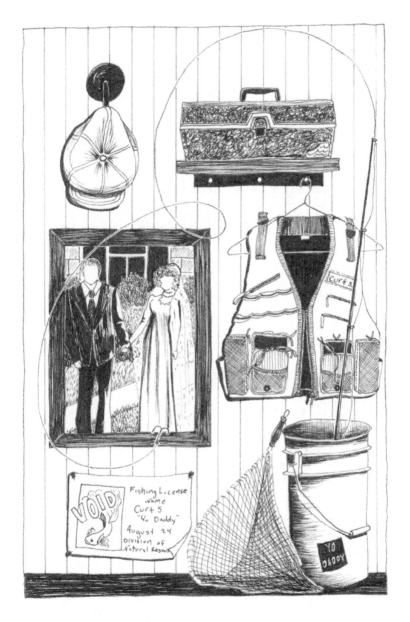

☐ In yo mama's house, ESPN stands for Excellent Spouses Provide Naps.

Yo daddy knows when to hand over the remote and take the kids outside.

☐ Yo mama's such a good driver you sometimes think she should drive for NASCAR.

If she did, imagine the sponsorship opportunities: chocolate, Diet Coke, chocolate, Clorox Wipes, chocolate, Panera, and chocolate just to name a few.

☐ Yo mama's so smart she has an answer for anything. Which is a good thing since you like to question everything.

☐ Yo mama and Indiana Jones have a lot in common. They've both fearlessly faced down rooms full of obstacles and dangerous traps (your room).

And yo mama hates snakes too.

☐ Yo mama loves you unconditionally...
on the condition that you call twice a week.

☐ Yo mama's so forgiving that it's more like FIVEgiving.

☐ Yo mama was so generous to take you on vacation when you were a kid. And she was so forgiving she let you come back home too.

☐ Yo mama was so patient with you as you learned to color inside the lines of your coloring book, and even more patient as you colored inside the lines of her furniture, drapes and wall.

☐ Yo mama's house is so clean you could eat spaghetti off the carpet.

☐ Yo mama's so patient she dealt with your mood swings about not wanting to get in the bath and then an hour later not wanting to get out.

☐   If yo mama ever wanted to join the Navy SEALs, they wouldn't need to send her to boot camp. They'd just need to ask her how many times she'd successfully taken kids somewhere on an airplane.

☐   Yo mama's so patient she waited until you were 25 to say "Told you so".

☐ Yo mama's so photogenic that her picture helped a DMV employee win a photo contest.

☐ Yo mama loves you so much that you realize now that when you helped her make dinner as a child, you were actually helping her take twice as long to make it.

☐ Yo mama's so loyal that after coming to your sports games she voluntarily served as a designated driver for a van full of seven-year-olds hyped up on Twinkies and juice boxes.

☐ Yo mama's so patient that she read you *Goodnight Moon* hundreds of times without complaining before reading even one of the books on her nightstand.

Sometimes she wondered if she'd become an old lady whispering "hush" before it happened.

☐ You may have noticed that you most appreciate yo mama when your life is upside down. While you're upside down, consider what the word "MOM" looks like and think "WOW, I have a great mama!".

☐ Yo mama thinks so highly of you that she never thought anyone you dated was ever good enough for you, even though they pretty much were.

☐ Yo mama's so efficient, she had twins.

☐ Yo mama's so frugal that when she goes to the movies she sneaks in her own popcorn *and* microwave.

☐ Yo mama's such an expert grocery shopper that she could always get her full list without you catching sight of the candy aisle even once.

☐ Yo mama's so magical that she could always make your Halloween costume appear in one night.

Then she could magically make all of your leftover Halloween candy disappear the next night.

☐ Yo mama's so good at multitasking that she just finished her Christmas shopping while reading this.

☐ Yo mama's so loving that you somehow made it on the "nice list" every Christmas even though yo mama had so much evidence to the contrary.

☐ Yo mama's so supportive that she paid for your music lessons *and* stayed indoors while you practiced.

79

☐ Yo mama's so patient she once played an entire game of Monopoly with you.

☐ Yo mama's so smart she taught you everything you know. But it's gonna be pretty hard for her to teach you everything *she* knows.

☐   Yo mama's so amazing. Period.

(This one's a fact, not a joke.)

ACKNOWLEDGMENTS

We'd like to thank the many people who helped make this book happen and who made it better with their feedback.

Biggest thanks to our spouses Meagan, Abby and Jimmy for providing the support and time we needed.

Thanks to our earliest readers, Joshua's kids, for laughing so generously and being so enthusiastic.

Thanks to our other early readers for helping us refine and pick the best of the jokes: the extended Swenson and Williams families, the Ences, the Sessions, and the McNeils.

Thanks to Joshua's writing group buddies for the great feedback on this and other projects: Elizabeth Dimit, Jared Agard, and Joshua Tomsik.

Joshua and Gibson are grateful to Megan for making some of their favorite jokes come to life so beautifully.

Lastly, thanks to mothers everywhere. You're the inspiration!

ABOUT THE AUTHORS

Joshua Swenson loves life with his lovely wife, Meagan, in beautiful Oregon. Together they have successfully invented four perpetual motion machines (two girls and two boys). Joshua was surprised to find out he actually liked writing as a senior in high school when he dropped out of honors English and took creative writing instead from a demanding and inspiring teacher. Since then, he has harbored a hope of writing professionally and is thrilled to launch this book as the first of several projects. You can connect with him at www.booktree.org.

A native of the San Francisco Bay Area, **Gibson Grey** now lives in Los Angeles with his wife and three children. He's written professionally for 15 years and has been published in both *Reader's Digest* and *Writer's Digest* magazines.

ABOUT THE ILLUSTRATOR

Megan Speirs Mack is an artist-mama of three, creating in Texas with her best friend-husband, Jimmy. She finds perspective and connection in the creative process and loves to honor and celebrate the beauty and intricacy of nature and humanity through the art she makes. Since graduating in 2008 with a BFA in Art and Visual Culture Education from the University of Arizona, she has guided hundreds of people on their journeys to find their own artistic voices. Megan thrives on the interactive and collaborative elements that enrich her work. She continues designing, illustrating, and creating fine art collections from her home studio, often with the company of one of her children busily working by her side.

meganspeirsmack.com

Made in the USA
Coppell, TX
07 May 2021